THIS Paranormal notebook

BELONGS TO:

_____

Investigation Date _____   Time _____

Address _____

Haunt Information

What happens?
Date of first experience
Description of events

Suspected entity information

Possible Names	Dates alive
Where entity lived	Entity's motives/wants
Story	

Investigation recordings

Site Temperature

Cold   Neutral   Hot

Atmosphere

Oppressive   Neutral   Light

Site observation

Sensory Notes

Equipment Used

Equipment	Readings

Investigation Date _____ Time _____

Address _____

Haunt Information

What happens?

Date of first experience

Description of events

Suspected entity information

Possible Names	Dates alive
Where entity lived	Entity's motives/wants
Story	

Investigation recordings

Site Temperature

Cold   Neutral   Hot

Atmosphere

Oppressive   Neutral   Light

Site observation

Sensory Notes

Equipment Used

Equipment	Readings

Investigation Date _____   Time _____

Address _____

Haunt Information

What happens?

Date of first experience

Description of events

Suspected entity information

Possible Names	Dates alive
Where entity lived	Entity's motives/wants
Story	

Investigation recordings

Site Temperature

Cold   Neutral   Hot

Atmosphere

Oppressive   Neutral   Light

Site observation

Sensory Notes

Equipment Used

Equipment	Readings

Investigation Date _____ Time _____

Address _____

Haunt Information

What happens?

Date of first experience

Description of events

Suspected entity information

Possible Names	Dates alive
Where entity lived	Entity's motives/wants
Story	

Investigation recordings

Site Temperature

Cold   Neutral   Hot

Atmosphere

Oppressive   Neutral   Light

Site observation

Sensory Notes

Equipment Used

Equipment	Readings

Investigation Date _____ Time _____

Address _____

Haunt Information

What happens?

Date of first experience

Description of events

Suspected entity information

Possible Names	Dates alive
Where entity lived	Entity's motives/wants
Story	

Investigation recordings

Site Temperature

Cold   Neutral   Hot

Atmosphere

Oppressive   Neutral   Light

Site observation

Sensory Notes

Equipment Used

Equipment	Readings

Investigation Date _____   Time _____

Address _____

Haunt Information

What happens?

Date of first experience

Description of events

Suspected entity information

Possible Names	Dates alive
Where entity lived	Entity's motives/wants
Story	

Investigation recordings

Site Temperature

Cold   Neutral   Hot

Atmosphere

Oppressive   Neutral   Light

Site observation

Sensory Notes

Equipment Used

Equipment	Readings

Investigation Date _____ Time _____

Address _____

Haunt Information

What happens?

Date of first experience

Description of events

Suspected entity information

Possible Names	Dates alive
Where entity lived	Entity's motives/wants
Story	

Investigation recordings

Site Temperature

Cold   Neutral   Hot

Atmosphere

Oppressive   Neutral   Light

Site observation

Sensory Notes

Equipment Used

Equipment	Readings

Investigation Date _____ Time _____

Address _____

Haunt Information

What happens?

Date of first experience

Description of events

Suspected entity information

Possible Names	Dates alive
Where entity lived	Entity's motives/wants
Story	

Investigation recordings

Site Temperature

Cold   Neutral   Hot

Atmosphere

Oppressive   Neutral   Light

Site observation

Sensory Notes

Equipment Used

Equipment	Readings

Investigation Date _____   Time _____

Address _____

Haunt Information

What happens?

Date of first experience

Description of events

Suspected entity information

Possible Names   Dates alive

Where entity lived   Entity's motives/wants

Story

Investigation recordings

Site Temperature

Cold   Neutral   Hot

Atmosphere

Oppressive   Neutral   Light

Site observation

Sensory Notes

Equipment Used

Equipment	Readings

Investigation Date _____ Time _____

Address _____

Haunt Information

What happens?

Date of first experience

Description of events

Suspected entity information

Possible Names	Dates alive
Where entity lived	Entity's motives/wants
Story	

Investigation recordings

Site Temperature

Cold   Neutral   Hot

Atmosphere

Oppressive   Neutral   Light

Site observation

Sensory Notes

Equipment Used

Equipment	Readings

Investigation Date _____   Time _____

Address _____

Haunt Information

What happens?

Date of first experience

Description of events

Suspected entity information

Possible Names   Dates alive

Where entity lived   Entity's motives/wants

Story

Investigation recordings

Site Temperature

Cold   Neutral   Hot

Atmosphere

Oppressive   Neutral   Light

Site observation

Sensory Notes

Equipment Used

Equipment	Readings

Investigation Date _____ Time _____

Address _____

Haunt Information

What happens?

Date of first experience

Description of events

Suspected entity information

Possible Names	Dates alive
Where entity lived	Entity's motives/wants
Story	

Investigation recordings

Site Temperature

Cold   Neutral   Hot

Atmosphere

Oppressive   Neutral   Light

Site observation

Sensory Notes

Equipment Used

Equipment	Readings

Investigation Date _____ Time _____

Address _____

Haunt Information

What happens?

Date of first experience

Description of events

Suspected entity information

Possible Names   Dates alive

Where entity lived   Entity's motives/wants

Story

Investigation recordings

Site Temperature

Cold   Neutral   Hot

Atmosphere

Oppressive   Neutral   Light

Site observation

Sensory Notes

Equipment Used

Equipment	Readings

Investigation Date _____   Time _____

Address _____

Haunt Information

What happens?
Date of first experience
Description of events

Suspected entity information

Possible Names	Dates alive
Where entity lived	Entity's motives/wants
Story	

Investigation recordings

Site Temperature

Cold   Neutral   Hot

Atmosphere

Oppressive   Neutral   Light

Site observation

Sensory Notes

Equipment Used

Equipment	Readings

Investigation Date _____ Time _____

Address _____

Haunt Information

What happens?

Date of first experience

Description of events

Suspected entity information

Possible Names	Dates alive
Where entity lived	Entity's motives/wants
Story	

Investigation recordings

Site Temperature

Cold   Neutral   Hot

Atmosphere

Oppressive   Neutral   Light

Site observation

Sensory Notes

Equipment Used

Equipment	Readings

Investigation Date _____ Time _____

Address _____

Haunt Information

What happens?

Date of first experience

Description of events

Suspected entity information

Possible Names   Dates alive

Where entity lived   Entity's motives/wants

Story

Investigation recordings

Site Temperature

Cold   Neutral   Hot

Atmosphere

Oppressive   Neutral   Light

Site observation

Sensory Notes

Equipment Used

Equipment	Readings

Investigation Date _____   Time _____

Address _____

Haunt Information

What happens?

Date of first experience

Description of events

Suspected entity information

Possible Names	Dates alive
Where entity lived	Entity's motives/wants
Story	

Investigation recordings

Site Temperature

Cold   Neutral   Hot

Atmosphere

Oppressive   Neutral   Light

Site observation

Sensory Notes

Equipment Used

Equipment	Readings

Investigation Date _____ Time _____

Address _____

Haunt Information

What happens?

Date of first experience

Description of events

Suspected entity information

Possible Names	Dates alive
Where entity lived	Entity's motives/wants
Story	

Investigation recordings

Site Temperature

Cold   Neutral   Hot

Atmosphere

Oppressive   Neutral   Light

Site observation

Sensory Notes

Equipment Used

Equipment	Readings

Investigation Date _____   Time _____

Address _____

Haunt Information

What happens?

Date of first experience

Description of events

Suspected entity information

Possible Names	Dates alive
Where entity lived	Entity's motives/wants
Story	

Investigation recordings

Site Temperature

Cold   Neutral   Hot

Atmosphere

Oppressive   Neutral   Light

Site observation

Sensory Notes

Equipment Used

Equipment	Readings

Investigation Date _____   Time _____

Address _____

Haunt Information

What happens?

Date of first experience

Description of events

Suspected entity information

Possible Names	Dates alive
Where entity lived	Entity's motives/wants
Story	

Investigation recordings

Site Temperature

Cold   Neutral   Hot

Atmosphere

Oppressive   Neutral   Light

Site observation

Sensory Notes

Equipment Used

Equipment	Readings

Investigation Date _____   Time _____

Address _____

Haunt Information

What happens?

Date of first experience

Description of events

Suspected entity information

Possible Names	Dates alive
Where entity lived	Entity's motives/wants
Story	

Investigation recordings

Site Temperature

Cold   Neutral   Hot

Atmosphere

Oppressive   Neutral   Light

Site observation

Sensory Notes

Equipment Used

Equipment	Readings

Investigation Date _____ Time _____

Address _____

Haunt Information

What happens?

Date of first experience

Description of events

Suspected entity information

Possible Names	Dates alive
Where entity lived	Entity's motives/wants
Story	

Investigation recordings

Site Temperature

Cold   Neutral   Hot

Atmosphere

Oppressive   Neutral   Light

Site observation

Sensory Notes

Equipment Used

Equipment	Readings

Investigation Date _____ Time _____

Address _____

Haunt Information

What happens?

Date of first experience

Description of events

Suspected entity information

Possible Names	Dates alive
Where entity lived	Entity's motives/wants
Story	

Investigation recordings

Site Temperature

Cold   Neutral   Hot

Atmosphere

Oppressive   Neutral   Light

Site observation

Sensory Notes

Equipment Used

Equipment	Readings

Investigation Date _____ Time _____

Address _____

Haunt Information

What happens?

Date of first experience

Description of events

Suspected entity information

| Possible Names | Dates alive |

Where entity lived

Entity's motives/wants

Story

Investigation recordings

Site Temperature

Cold   Neutral   Hot

Atmosphere

Oppressive   Neutral   Light

Site observation

Sensory Notes

Equipment Used

Equipment	Readings

Investigation Date _____ Time _____

Address _____

Haunt Information

What happens?

Date of first experience

Description of events

Suspected entity information

Possible Names	Dates alive
Where entity lived	Entity's motives/wants
Story	

Investigation recordings

Site Temperature

Cold   Neutral   Hot

Atmosphere

Oppressive   Neutral   Light

Site observation

Sensory Notes

Equipment Used

Equipment	Readings

Investigation Date _____   Time _____

Address _____

Haunt Information

What happens?

Date of first experience

Description of events

Suspected entity information

Possible Names   Dates alive

Where entity lived   Entity's motives/wants

Story

Investigation recordings

Site Temperature										

Cold   Neutral   Hot

Atmosphere										

Oppressive   Neutral   Light

Site observation

Sensory Notes

Equipment Used

Equipment	Readings

Investigation Date _____ Time _____

Address _____

Haunt Information

What happens?

Date of first experience

Description of events

Suspected entity information

Possible Names	Dates alive
Where entity lived	Entity's motives/wants
Story	

Investigation recordings

Site Temperature

Cold   Neutral   Hot

Atmosphere

Oppressive   Neutral   Light

Site observation

Sensory Notes

Equipment Used

Equipment	Readings

Investigation Date _____ Time _____

Address _____

Haunt Information

What happens?

Date of first experience

Description of events

Suspected entity information

Possible Names   Dates alive

Where entity lived   Entity's motives/wants

Story

Investigation recordings

Site Temperature

Cold   Neutral   Hot

Atmosphere

Oppressive   Neutral   Light

Site observation

Sensory Notes

Equipment Used

Equipment	Readings

Investigation Date _____   Time _____

Address _____

Haunt Information

What happens?

Date of first experience

Description of events

Suspected entity information

Possible Names	Dates alive
Where entity lived	Entity's motives/wants
Story	

Investigation recordings

Site Temperature

Cold   Neutral   Hot

Atmosphere

Oppressive   Neutral   Light

Site observation

Sensory Notes

Equipment Used

Equipment	Readings

Investigation Date _____ Time _____

Address _____

Haunt Information

What happens?

Date of first experience

Description of events

Suspected entity information

Possible Names	Dates alive
Where entity lived	Entity's motives/wants
Story	

Investigation recordings

Site Temperature

Cold   Neutral   Hot

Atmosphere

Oppressive   Neutral   Light

Site observation

Sensory Notes

Equipment Used

Equipment	Readings

Investigation Date _____ Time _____

Address _____

Haunt Information

What happens?

Date of first experience

Description of events

Suspected entity information

Possible Names	Dates alive
Where entity lived	Entity's motives/wants
Story	

Investigation recordings

Site Temperature

Cold   Neutral   Hot

Atmosphere

Oppressive   Neutral   Light

Site observation

Sensory Notes

Equipment Used

Equipment	Readings

Investigation Date _____ Time _____

Address _____

Haunt Information

What happens?

Date of first experience

Description of events

Suspected entity information

Possible Names	Dates alive
Where entity lived	Entity's motives/wants
Story	

Investigation recordings

Site Temperature

Cold   Neutral   Hot

Atmosphere

Oppressive   Neutral   Light

Site observation

Sensory Notes

Equipment Used

Equipment	Readings

Investigation Date _____ Time _____

Address _____

Haunt Information

What happens?

Date of first experience

Description of events

Suspected entity information

Possible Names	Dates alive
Where entity lived	Entity's motives/wants
Story	

Investigation recordings

Site Temperature

Cold   Neutral   Hot

Atmosphere

Oppressive   Neutral   Light

Site observation

Sensory Notes

Equipment Used

Equipment	Readings

Investigation Date _____   Time _____

Address _____

Haunt Information

What happens?

Date of first experience

Description of events

Suspected entity information

Possible Names   Dates alive

Where entity lived   Entity's motives/wants

Story

Investigation recordings

Site Temperature

Cold   Neutral   Hot

Atmosphere

Oppressive   Neutral   Light

Site observation

Sensory Notes

Equipment Used

Equipment	Readings

Investigation Date _____   Time _____

Address _____

Haunt Information

What happens?

Date of first experience

Description of events

Suspected entity information

Possible Names	Dates alive
Where entity lived	Entity's motives/wants
Story	

Investigation recordings

Site Temperature

Cold   Neutral   Hot

Atmosphere

Oppressive   Neutral   Light

Site observation

Sensory Notes

Equipment Used

Equipment	Readings

Investigation Date _____ Time _____

Address _____

Haunt Information

What happens?

Date of first experience

Description of events

Suspected entity information

Possible Names	Dates alive
Where entity lived	Entity's motives/wants
Story	

Investigation recordings

Site Temperature

Cold   Neutral   Hot

Atmosphere

Oppressive   Neutral   Light

Site observation

Sensory Notes

Equipment Used

Equipment	Readings

Investigation Date _____   Time _____

Address _____

Haunt Information

What happens?

Date of first experience

Description of events

Suspected entity information

Possible Names   Dates alive

Where entity lived   Entity's motives/wants

Story

Investigation recordings

Site Temperature

Cold					Neutral				Hot

Atmosphere

Oppressive					Neutral				Light

Site observation

Sensory Notes

Equipment Used

Equipment	Readings

Investigation Date _____ Time _____

Address _____

Haunt Information

What happens?
Date of first experience
Description of events

Suspected entity information

Possible Names	Dates alive
Where entity lived	Entity's motives/wants
Story	

Investigation recordings

Site Temperature

Cold   Neutral   Hot

Atmosphere

Oppressive   Neutral   Light

Site observation

Sensory Notes

Equipment Used

Equipment	Readings

Investigation Date _____ Time _____

Address _____

Haunt Information

What happens?

Date of first experience

Description of events

Suspected entity information

Possible Names   Dates alive

Where entity lived   Entity's motives/wants

Story

Investigation recordings

Site Temperature

Cold   Neutral   Hot

Atmosphere

Oppressive   Neutral   Light

Site observation

Sensory Notes

Equipment Used

Equipment	Readings

Investigation Date _____ Time _____

Address _____

Haunt Information

What happens?

Date of first experience

Description of events

Suspected entity information

Possible Names   Dates alive

Where entity lived   Entity's motives/wants

Story

Investigation recordings

Site Temperature

Cold   Neutral   Hot

Atmosphere

Oppressive   Neutral   Light

Site observation

Sensory Notes

Equipment Used

Equipment	Readings

Investigation Date _____   Time _____

Address _____

Haunt Information

What happens?

Date of first experience

Description of events

Suspected entity information

Possible Names	Dates alive
Where entity lived	Entity's motives/wants
Story	

Investigation recordings

Site Temperature

Cold   Neutral   Hot

Atmosphere

Oppressive   Neutral   Light

Site observation

Sensory Notes

Equipment Used

Equipment	Readings

Investigation Date _____ Time _____

Address _____

Haunt Information

What happens?

Date of first experience

Description of events

Suspected entity information

Possible Names   Dates alive

Where entity lived   Entity's motives/wants

Story

Investigation recordings

Site Temperature

Cold   Neutral   Hot

Atmosphere

Oppressive   Neutral   Light

Site observation

Sensory Notes

Equipment Used

Equipment	Readings

Investigation Date _____ Time _____

Address _____

Haunt Information

What happens?

Date of first experience

Description of events

Suspected entity information

Possible Names   Dates alive

Where entity lived   Entity's motives/wants

Story

Investigation recordings

Site Temperature
Cold   Neutral   Hot

Atmosphere
Oppressive   Neutral   Light

Site observation

Sensory Notes

Equipment Used

Equipment	Readings

Investigation Date _____ Time _____

Address _____

Haunt Information

What happens?

Date of first experience

Description of events

Suspected entity information

Possible Names	Dates alive
Where entity lived	Entity's motives/wants
Story	

Investigation recordings

Site Temperature

Cold   Neutral   Hot

Atmosphere

Oppressive   Neutral   Light

Site observation

Sensory Notes

Equipment Used

Equipment	Readings

Investigation Date _____ Time _____

Address _____

Haunt Information

What happens?

Date of first experience

Description of events

Suspected entity information

Possible Names	Dates alive
Where entity lived	Entity's motives/wants
Story	

Investigation recordings

Site Temperature

Cold   Neutral   Hot

Atmosphere

Oppressive   Neutral   Light

Site observation

Sensory Notes

Equipment Used

Equipment	Readings

Investigation Date _____ Time _____

Address _____

Haunt Information

What happens?

Date of first experience

Description of events

Suspected entity information

Possible Names	Dates alive
Where entity lived	Entity's motives/wants
Story	

Investigation recordings

Site Temperature

Cold   Neutral   Hot

Atmosphere

Oppressive   Neutral   Light

Site observation

Sensory Notes

Equipment Used

Equipment	Readings

Investigation Date _____   Time _____

Address _____

Haunt Information

What happens?

Date of first experience

Description of events

Suspected entity information

Possible Names	Dates alive
Where entity lived	Entity's motives/wants
Story	

Investigation recordings

Site Temperature

Cold   Neutral   Hot

Atmosphere

Oppressive   Neutral   Light

Site observation

Sensory Notes

Equipment Used

Equipment	Readings

Investigation Date _____ Time _____

Address _____

Haunt Information

What happens?

Date of first experience

Description of events

Suspected entity information

Possible Names	Dates alive
Where entity lived	Entity's motives/wants
Story	

Investigation recordings

Site Temperature

Cold   Neutral   Hot

Atmosphere

Oppressive   Neutral   Light

Site observation

Sensory Notes

Equipment Used

Equipment	Readings

Investigation Date _____ Time _____

Address _____

Haunt Information

What happens?

Date of first experience

Description of events

Suspected entity information

Possible Names   Dates alive

Where entity lived   Entity's motives/wants

Story

Investigation recordings

Site Temperature

Cold   Neutral   Hot

Atmosphere

Oppressive   Neutral   Light

Site observation

Sensory Notes

Equipment Used

Equipment	Readings

Investigation Date _____   Time _____

Address _____

Haunt Information

What happens?

Date of first experience

Description of events

Suspected entity information

Possible Names   Dates alive

Where entity lived   Entity's motives/wants

Story

Investigation recordings

Site Temperature

Cold   Neutral   Hot

Atmosphere

Oppressive   Neutral   Light

Site observation

Sensory Notes

Equipment Used

Equipment	Readings

Investigation Date _____ Time _____

Address _____

Haunt Information

What happens?

Date of first experience

Description of events

Suspected entity information

Possible Names	Dates alive
Where entity lived	Entity's motives/wants
Story	

Investigation recordings

Site Temperature

Cold   Neutral   Hot

Atmosphere

Oppressive   Neutral   Light

Site observation

Sensory Notes

Equipment Used

Equipment	Readings

Investigation Date _____ Time _____

Address _____

Haunt Information

What happens?

Date of first experience

Description of events

Suspected entity information

Possible Names	Dates alive
Where entity lived	Entity's motives/wants
Story	

Investigation recordings

Site Temperature

Cold   Neutral   Hot

Atmosphere

Oppressive   Neutral   Light

Site observation

Sensory Notes

Equipment Used

Equipment	Readings

Investigation Date _____ Time _____

Address _____

Haunt Information

What happens?

Date of first experience

Description of events

Suspected entity information

Possible Names	Dates alive
Where entity lived	Entity's motives/wants
Story	

Investigation recordings

Site Temperature

Cold   Neutral   Hot

Atmosphere

Oppressive   Neutral   Light

Site observation

Sensory Notes

Equipment Used

Equipment	Readings

Investigation Date _____   Time _____

Address _____

Haunt Information

What happens?

Date of first experience

Description of events

Suspected entity information

Possible Names   Dates alive

Where entity lived   Entity's motives/wants

Story

Investigation recordings

Site Temperature

Cold   Neutral   Hot

Atmosphere

Oppressive   Neutral   Light

Site observation

Sensory Notes

Equipment Used

Equipment	Readings

Investigation Date _____ Time _____

Address _____

Haunt Information

What happens?

Date of first experience

Description of events

Suspected entity information

Possible Names   Dates alive

Where entity lived   Entity's motives/wants

Story

Investigation recordings

Site Temperature

Cold   Neutral   Hot

Atmosphere

Oppressive   Neutral   Light

Site observation

Sensory Notes

Equipment Used

Equipment	Readings

Investigation Date _____   Time _____

Address _____

Haunt Information

What happens?

Date of first experience

Description of events

Suspected entity information

Possible Names	Dates alive
Where entity lived	Entity's motives/wants
Story	

Investigation recordings

Site Temperature

Cold   Neutral   Hot

Atmosphere

Oppressive   Neutral   Light

Site observation

Sensory Notes

Equipment Used

Equipment	Readings

Investigation Date _____ Time _____

Address _____

Haunt Information

What happens?

Date of first experience

Description of events

Suspected entity information

Possible Names	Dates alive
Where entity lived	Entity's motives/wants
Story	

Investigation recordings

Site Temperature

Cold · · · · · · · Neutral · · · · · · · Hot

Atmosphere

Oppressive · · · · · Neutral · · · · · Light

Site observation

Sensory Notes

Equipment Used

Equipment	Readings

Investigation Date _____ Time _____

Address _____

Haunt Information

What happens?

Date of first experience

Description of events

Suspected entity information

Possible Names	Dates alive
Where entity lived	Entity's motives/wants

Story

Investigation recordings

Site Temperature

Cold   Neutral   Hot

Atmosphere

Oppressive   Neutral   Light

Site observation

Sensory Notes

Equipment Used

Equipment	Readings

Investigation Date _____ Time _____

Address _____

Haunt Information

What happens?

Date of first experience

Description of events

Suspected entity information

Possible Names	Dates alive
Where entity lived	Entity's motives/wants
Story	

Investigation recordings

Site Temperature

Cold   Neutral   Hot

Atmosphere

Oppressive   Neutral   Light

Site observation

Sensory Notes

Equipment Used

Equipment	Readings

Investigation Date _____ Time _____

Address _____

Haunt Information

What happens?

Date of first experience

Description of events

Suspected entity information

Possible Names	Dates alive
Where entity lived	Entity's motives/wants

Story

Investigation recordings

Site Temperature

Cold   Neutral   Hot

Atmosphere

Oppressive   Neutral   Light

Site observation

Sensory Notes

Equipment Used

Equipment	Readings

Investigation Date _____   Time _____

Address _____

Haunt Information

What happens?

Date of first experience

Description of events

Suspected entity information

Possible Names	Dates alive
Where entity lived	Entity's motives/wants
Story	

Investigation recordings

Site Temperature

Cold   Neutral   Hot

Atmosphere

Oppressive   Neutral   Light

Site observation

Sensory Notes

Equipment Used

Equipment	Readings

Investigation Date _____ Time _____

Address _____

Haunt Information

What happens?

Date of first experience

Description of events

Suspected entity information

Possible Names	Dates alive
Where entity lived	Entity's motives/wants
Story	

Investigation recordings

Site Temperature

Cold   Neutral   Hot

Atmosphere

Oppressive   Neutral   Light

Site observation

Sensory Notes

Equipment Used

Equipment	Readings

Investigation Date _____   Time _____

Address _____

Haunt Information

What happens?

Date of first experience

Description of events

Suspected entity information

Possible Names   Dates alive

Where entity lived   Entity's motives/wants

Story

Investigation recordings

Site Temperature

Cold   Neutral   Hot

Atmosphere

Oppressive   Neutral   Light

Site observation

Sensory Notes

Equipment Used

Equipment	Readings

Investigation Date _____   Time _____

Address _____

Haunt Information

What happens?

Date of first experience

Description of events

Suspected entity information

Possible Names	Dates alive
Where entity lived	Entity's motives/wants
Story	

Investigation recordings

Site Temperature

Cold   Neutral   Hot

Atmosphere

Oppressive   Neutral   Light

Site observation

Sensory Notes

Equipment Used

Equipment	Readings

Investigation Date _____   Time _____

Address _____

Haunt Information

What happens?

Date of first experience

Description of events

Suspected entity information

Possible Names   Dates alive

Where entity lived   Entity's motives/wants

Story

Investigation recordings

Site Temperature

Cold   Neutral   Hot

Atmosphere

Oppressive   Neutral   Light

Site observation

Sensory Notes

Equipment Used

Equipment	Readings

Investigation Date _____ Time _____

Address _____

Haunt Information

What happens?

Date of first experience

Description of events

Suspected entity information

Possible Names	Dates alive
Where entity lived	Entity's motives/wants
Story	

Investigation recordings

Site Temperature

Cold · · · · · · · · · · · Neutral · · · · · · · · · · · Hot

Atmosphere

Oppressive · · · · · · · · · Neutral · · · · · · · · · Light

Site observation

Sensory Notes

Equipment Used

Equipment	Readings

Investigation Date _____ Time _____

Address _____

Haunt Information

What happens?

Date of first experience

Description of events

Suspected entity information

Possible Names	Dates alive
Where entity lived	Entity's motives/wants
Story	

Investigation recordings

Site Temperature

Cold   Neutral   Hot

Atmosphere

Oppressive   Neutral   Light

Site observation

Sensory Notes

Equipment Used

Equipment	Readings

Investigation Date _____ Time _____

Address _____

Haunt Information

What happens?

Date of first experience

Description of events

Suspected entity information

Possible Names   Dates alive

Where entity lived   Entity's motives/wants

Story

Investigation recordings

Site Temperature

Cold   Neutral   Hot

Atmosphere

Oppressive   Neutral   Light

Site observation

Sensory Notes

Equipment Used

Equipment	Readings

Investigation Date _____ Time _____

Address _____

Haunt Information

What happens?

Date of first experience

Description of events

Suspected entity information

Possible Names	Dates alive
Where entity lived	Entity's motives/wants
Story	

Investigation recordings

Site Temperature

Cold   Neutral   Hot

Atmosphere

Oppressive   Neutral   Light

Site observation

Sensory Notes

Equipment Used

Equipment	Readings

Investigation Date _____   Time _____

Address _____

Haunt Information

What happens?

Date of first experience

Description of events

Suspected entity information

Possible Names	Dates alive
Where entity lived	Entity's motives/wants
Story	

Investigation recordings

Site Temperature

Cold   Neutral   Hot

Atmosphere

Oppressive   Neutral   Light

Site observation

Sensory Notes

Equipment Used

Equipment	Readings

Investigation Date _____ Time _____

Address _____

Haunt Information

What happens?

Date of first experience

Description of events

Suspected entity information

Possible Names	Dates alive
Where entity lived	Entity's motives/wants
Story	

Investigation recordings

Site Temperature

Cold   Neutral   Hot

Atmosphere

Oppressive   Neutral   Light

Site observation

Sensory Notes

Equipment Used

Equipment	Readings

Investigation Date _____   Time _____

Address _____

Haunt Information

What happens?

Date of first experience

Description of events

Suspected entity information

Possible Names   Dates alive

Where entity lived   Entity's motives/wants

Story

Investigation recordings

Site Temperature

Cold   Neutral   Hot

Atmosphere

Oppressive   Neutral   Light

Site observation

Sensory Notes

Equipment Used

Equipment	Readings

Investigation Date _____   Time _____

Address _____

Haunt Information

What happens?

Date of first experience

Description of events

Suspected entity information

Possible Names   Dates alive

Where entity lived   Entity's motives/wants

Story

Investigation recordings

Site Temperature

Cold   Neutral   Hot

Atmosphere

Oppressive   Neutral   Light

Site observation

Sensory Notes

Equipment Used

Equipment	Readings

Investigation Date _____   Time _____

Address _____

Haunt Information

What happens?

Date of first experience

Description of events

Suspected entity information

Possible Names	Dates alive
Where entity lived	Entity's motives/wants
Story	

Investigation recordings

Site Temperature

Cold   Neutral   Hot

Atmosphere

Oppressive   Neutral   Light

Site observation

Sensory Notes

Equipment Used

Equipment	Readings

Investigation Date _____ Time _____

Address _____

Haunt Information

What happens?

Date of first experience

Description of events

Suspected entity information

Possible Names	Dates alive
Where entity lived	Entity's motives/wants
Story	

Investigation recordings

Site Temperature

Cold　　　　　　　　　　　Neutral　　　　　　　　　　Hot

Atmosphere

Oppressive　　　　　　　　Neutral　　　　　　　　Light

Site observation

Sensory Notes

Equipment Used

Equipment	Readings

Investigation Date _____ Time _____

Address _____

Haunt Information

What happens?

Date of first experience

Description of events

Suspected entity information

Possible Names   Dates alive

Where entity lived   Entity's motives/wants

Story

Investigation recordings

Site Temperature

Cold   Neutral   Hot

Atmosphere

Oppressive   Neutral   Light

Site observation

Sensory Notes

Equipment Used

Equipment	Readings

Investigation Date _____ Time _____

Address _____

Haunt Information

What happens?

Date of first experience

Description of events

Suspected entity information

Possible Names	Dates alive
Where entity lived	Entity's motives/wants
Story	

Investigation recordings

Site Temperature

Cold   Neutral   Hot

Atmosphere

Oppressive   Neutral   Light

Site observation

Sensory Notes

Equipment Used

Equipment	Readings

Investigation Date _____   Time _____

Address _____

Haunt Information

What happens?

Date of first experience

Description of events

Suspected entity information

Possible Names	Dates alive
Where entity lived	Entity's motives/wants
Story	

Investigation recordings

Site Temperature

Cold   Neutral   Hot

Atmosphere

Oppressive   Neutral   Light

Site observation

Sensory Notes

Equipment Used

Equipment	Readings

Investigation Date _____   Time _____

Address _____

Haunt Information

What happens?

Date of first experience

Description of events

Suspected entity information

Possible Names	Dates alive
Where entity lived	Entity's motives/wants
Story	

Investigation recordings

Site Temperature

Cold   Neutral   Hot

Atmosphere

Oppressive   Neutral   Light

Site observation

Sensory Notes

Equipment Used

Equipment	Readings

Investigation Date _____   Time _____

Address _____

Haunt Information

What happens?

Date of first experience

Description of events

Suspected entity information

Possible Names   Dates alive

Where entity lived   Entity's motives/wants

Story

Investigation recordings

Site Temperature

Cold   Neutral   Hot

Atmosphere

Oppressive   Neutral   Light

Site observation

Sensory Notes

Equipment Used

Equipment	Readings

Investigation Date _____ Time _____

Address _____

Haunt Information

What happens?

Date of first experience

Description of events

Suspected entity information

Possible Names	Dates alive
Where entity lived	Entity's motives/wants
Story	

Investigation recordings

Site Temperature

Cold   Neutral   Hot

Atmosphere

Oppressive   Neutral   Light

Site observation

Sensory Notes

Equipment Used

Equipment	Readings

Investigation Date _____ Time _____

Address _____

Haunt Information

What happens?

Date of first experience

Description of events

Suspected entity information

Possible Names   Dates alive

Where entity lived   Entity's motives/wants

Story

Investigation recordings

Site Temperature

Cold   Neutral   Hot

Atmosphere

Oppressive   Neutral   Light

Site observation

Sensory Notes

Equipment Used

Equipment	Readings

Investigation Date _____   Time _____

Address _____

Haunt Information

What happens?

Date of first experience

Description of events

Suspected entity information

Possible Names   Dates alive

Where entity lived   Entity's motives/wants

Story

Investigation recordings

Site Temperature
Cold   Neutral   Hot

Atmosphere
Oppressive   Neutral   Light

Site observation

Sensory Notes

Equipment Used

Equipment	Readings

Investigation Date _____   Time _____

Address _____

Haunt Information

What happens?

Date of first experience

Description of events

Suspected entity information

Possible Names   Dates alive

Where entity lived   Entity's motives/wants

Story

Investigation recordings

Site Temperature | | | | | | | | | | |

Cold   Neutral   Hot

Atmosphere | | | | | | | | | | |

Oppressive   Neutral   Light

Site observation

Sensory Notes

Equipment Used

Equipment	Readings

Investigation Date _____ Time _____

Address _____

Haunt Information

What happens?

Date of first experience

Description of events

Suspected entity information

Possible Names   Dates alive

Where entity lived   Entity's motives/wants

Story

Investigation recordings

Site Temperature

Cold   Neutral   Hot

Atmosphere

Oppressive   Neutral   Light

Site observation

Sensory Notes

Equipment Used

Equipment	Readings

Investigation Date _____ Time _____

Address _____

Haunt Information

What happens?

Date of first experience

Description of events

Suspected entity information

| Possible Names | Dates alive |

Where entity lived

Entity's motives/wants

Story

Investigation recordings

Site Temperature

Cold   Neutral   Hot

Atmosphere

Oppressive   Neutral   Light

Site observation

Sensory Notes

Equipment Used

Equipment	Readings

Investigation Date _____ Time _____

Address _____

Haunt Information

What happens?

Date of first experience

Description of events

Suspected entity information

Possible Names	Dates alive
Where entity lived	Entity's motives/wants
Story	

Investigation recordings

Site Temperature

Cold   Neutral   Hot

Atmosphere

Oppressive   Neutral   Light

Site observation

Sensory Notes

Equipment Used

Equipment	Readings

Investigation Date _____ Time _____

Address _____

Haunt Information

What happens?

Date of first experience

Description of events

Suspected entity information

Possible Names   Dates alive

Where entity lived   Entity's motives/wants

Story

Investigation recordings

Site Temperature | | | | | | | | | | |

Cold   Neutral   Hot

Atmosphere | | | | | | | | | | |

Oppressive   Neutral   Light

Site observation

Sensory Notes

Equipment Used

Equipment	Readings

Investigation Date _____   Time _____

Address _____

Haunt Information

What happens?

Date of first experience

Description of events

Suspected entity information

Possible Names	Dates alive
Where entity lived	Entity's motives/wants
Story	

Investigation recordings

Site Temperature

Cold   Neutral   Hot

Atmosphere

Oppressive   Neutral   Light

Site observation

Sensory Notes

Equipment Used

Equipment	Readings

Investigation Date _____   Time _____

Address _____

Haunt Information

What happens?

Date of first experience

Description of events

Suspected entity information

Possible Names	Dates alive
Where entity lived	Entity's motives/wants

Story

Investigation recordings

Site Temperature

Cold   Neutral   Hot

Atmosphere

Oppressive   Neutral   Light

Site observation

Sensory Notes

Equipment Used

Equipment	Readings

Investigation Date _____ Time _____

Address _____

Haunt Information

What happens?

Date of first experience

Description of events

Suspected entity information

Possible Names   Dates alive

Where entity lived   Entity's motives/wants

Story

Investigation recordings

Site Temperature

Cold   Neutral   Hot

Atmosphere

Oppressive   Neutral   Light

Site observation

Sensory Notes

Equipment Used

Equipment	Readings

Investigation Date _____   Time _____

Address _____

Haunt Information

What happens?

Date of first experience

Description of events

Suspected entity information

Possible Names	Dates alive
Where entity lived	Entity's motives/wants
Story	

Investigation recordings

Site Temperature

Cold   Neutral   Hot

Atmosphere

Oppressive   Neutral   Light

Site observation

Sensory Notes

Equipment Used

Equipment	Readings

Investigation Date _____ Time _____

Address _____

Haunt Information

What happens?

Date of first experience

Description of events

Suspected entity information

Possible Names   Dates alive

Where entity lived   Entity's motives/wants

Story

Investigation recordings

Site Temperature

Cold   Neutral   Hot

Atmosphere

Oppressive   Neutral   Light

Site observation

Sensory Notes

Equipment Used

Equipment	Readings

Investigation Date _____ Time _____

Address _____

Haunt Information

What happens?

Date of first experience

Description of events

Suspected entity information

Possible Names	Dates alive
Where entity lived	Entity's motives/wants
Story	

Investigation recordings

Site Temperature

Cold   Neutral   Hot

Atmosphere

Oppressive   Neutral   Light

Site observation

Sensory Notes

Equipment Used

Equipment	Readings

Investigation Date _____ Time _____

Address _____

Haunt Information

What happens?

Date of first experience

Description of events

Suspected entity information

Possible Names   Dates alive

Where entity lived   Entity's motives/wants

Story

Investigation recordings

Site Temperature

Cold   Neutral   Hot

Atmosphere

Oppressive   Neutral   Light

Site observation

Sensory Notes

Equipment Used

Equipment	Readings

Investigation Date _____   Time _____

Address _____

Haunt Information

What happens?

Date of first experience

Description of events

Suspected entity information

Possible Names	Dates alive
Where entity lived	Entity's motives/wants
Story	

Investigation recordings

Site Temperature

Cold   Neutral   Hot

Atmosphere

Oppressive   Neutral   Light

Site observation

Sensory Notes

Equipment Used

Equipment	Readings

Investigation Date _____   Time _____

Address _____

Haunt Information

What happens?

Date of first experience

Description of events

Suspected entity information

Possible Names   Dates alive

Where entity lived   Entity's motives/wants

Story

Investigation recordings

Site Temperature

Cold   Neutral   Hot

Atmosphere

Oppressive   Neutral   Light

Site observation

Sensory Notes

Equipment Used

Equipment	Readings

Investigation Date _____ Time _____

Address _____

Haunt Information

What happens?

Date of first experience

Description of events

Suspected entity information

Possible Names	Dates alive
Where entity lived	Entity's motives/wants
Story	

Investigation recordings

Site Temperature

Cold   Neutral   Hot

Atmosphere

Oppressive   Neutral   Light

Site observation

Sensory Notes

Equipment Used

Equipment	Readings

Investigation Date _____   Time _____

Address _____

Haunt Information

What happens?

Date of first experience

Description of events

Suspected entity information

Possible Names	Dates alive
Where entity lived	Entity's motives/wants
Story	

Investigation recordings

Site Temperature

Cold   Neutral   Hot

Atmosphere

Oppressive   Neutral   Light

Site observation

Sensory Notes

Equipment Used

Equipment	Readings

Investigation Date _____ Time _____

Address _____

Haunt Information

What happens?

Date of first experience

Description of events

Suspected entity information

Possible Names   Dates alive

Where entity lived   Entity's motives/wants

Story

Investigation recordings

Site Temperature

Cold   Neutral   Hot

Atmosphere

Oppressive   Neutral   Light

Site observation

Sensory Notes

Equipment Used

Equipment	Readings

Investigation Date _____   Time _____

Address _____

Haunt Information

What happens?

Date of first experience

Description of events

Suspected entity information

| Possible Names | Dates alive |

Where entity lived   Entity's motives/wants

Story

Investigation recordings

Site Temperature

Cold   Neutral   Hot

Atmosphere

Oppressive   Neutral   Light

Site observation

Sensory Notes

Equipment Used

Equipment	Readings

Investigation Date _____ Time _____

Address _____

Haunt Information

What happens?

Date of first experience

Description of events

Suspected entity information

Possible Names   Dates alive

Where entity lived   Entity's motives/wants

Story

Investigation recordings

Site Temperature

Cold   Neutral   Hot

Atmosphere

Oppressive   Neutral   Light

Site observation

Sensory Notes

Equipment Used

Equipment	Readings

Investigation Date _____ Time _____

Address _____

Haunt Information

What happens?

Date of first experience

Description of events

Suspected entity information

Possible Names   Dates alive

Where entity lived   Entity's motives/wants

Story

Investigation recordings

Site Temperature

Cold   Neutral   Hot

Atmosphere

Oppressive   Neutral   Light

Site observation

Sensory Notes

Equipment Used

Equipment	Readings

Investigation Date _____   Time _____

Address _____

Haunt Information

What happens?

Date of first experience

Description of events

Suspected entity information

Possible Names	Dates alive
Where entity lived	Entity's motives/wants
Story	

Investigation recordings

Site Temperature

Cold   Neutral   Hot

Atmosphere

Oppressive   Neutral   Light

Site observation

Sensory Notes

Equipment Used

Equipment	Readings

Investigation Date _____ Time _____

Address _____

Haunt Information

What happens?

Date of first experience

Description of events

Suspected entity information

Possible Names	Dates alive
Where entity lived	Entity's motives/wants
Story	

Investigation recordings

Site Temperature

Cold   Neutral   Hot

Atmosphere

Oppressive   Neutral   Light

Site observation

Sensory Notes

Equipment Used

Equipment	Readings

Investigation Date _____   Time _____

Address _____

Haunt Information

What happens?

Date of first experience

Description of events

Suspected entity information

Possible Names   Dates alive

Where entity lived   Entity's motives/wants

Story

Investigation recordings

Site Temperature

Cold   Neutral   Hot

Atmosphere

Oppressive   Neutral   Light

Site observation

Sensory Notes

Equipment Used

Equipment	Readings

Investigation Date _____ Time _____

Address _____

Haunt Information

What happens?

Date of first experience

Description of events

Suspected entity information

Possible Names	Dates alive
Where entity lived	Entity's motives/wants
Story	

Investigation recordings

Site Temperature

Cold   Neutral   Hot

Atmosphere

Oppressive   Neutral   Light

Site observation

Sensory Notes

Equipment Used

Equipment	Readings

Investigation Date _____ Time _____

Address _____

Haunt Information

What happens?

Date of first experience

Description of events

Suspected entity information

Possible Names   Dates alive

Where entity lived   Entity's motives/wants

Story

Investigation recordings

Site Temperature

Cold   Neutral   Hot

Atmosphere

Oppressive   Neutral   Light

Site observation

Sensory Notes

Equipment Used

Equipment	Readings

Investigation Date _____ Time _____

Address _____

Haunt Information

What happens?

Date of first experience

Description of events

Suspected entity information

Possible Names   Dates alive

Where entity lived   Entity's motives/wants

Story

Investigation recordings

Site Temperature

Cold   Neutral   Hot

Atmosphere

Oppressive   Neutral   Light

Site observation

Sensory Notes

Equipment Used

Equipment	Readings

Made in the USA
Middletown, DE
25 October 2020